For Shelby and Dylan

First published in 2019 by Child's Play (International) Ltd
Ashworth Road, Bridgemead, Swindon SN5 7YD, UK

Published in USA by Child's Play Inc
250 Minot Avenue, Auburn, Maine 04210

Distributed in Australia by Child's Play Australia Pty Ltd
Unit 10/20 Narabang Way, Belrose, Sydney, NSW 2085

ISBN 978-1-78628-351-1
CLP290519CPL07193511

Printed in Shenzhen, China

1 3 5 7 9 10 8 6 4 2

A catalogue record of this book
is available from the British Library

www.childs-play.com

Milo AND Monty

ROXANA DE ROND

One sunny morning in May, Milo and Monty
came to live with the McKenzie family,
Mum, Sam and Lucy.

The puppies ate together,

slept together and...

had accidents together, too.

Monty liked to relax in the sun,

watch television with the family...

and play with
the other dogs in the park.

Monty would happily wag his tail,
nudge for more hugs and snuggle
up close when they cuddled him.

It was not the same with Milo.
Sometimes it was hard to know how he felt.
He hardly ever wagged his tail and growled
when they tried to hug him.

Milo found it hard to relax. When a car passed or a door slammed or when the wind blew too hard, Milo worried.

The family tried to comfort him, but when they stroked Milo's ears he shied away. And when they tried to hold him safe he looked nervous and upset.

They began to wonder if Milo was happy.

One Sunday afternoon
the cousins came to visit.
There was a lot of excited
chatter, and loud laughter.

Milo went in search of his favourite quiet spot.

But someone was already there!

It was cousin Henry.

Everyone had a great time.

Later that evening the McKenzies
talked about their day.

"Did you notice
how Milo and Henry
both like to find a quiet,
cosy place?" asked Mum.

"Henry has a special toy that he takes everywhere, just like Milo," said Sam.

"They both enjoy being near us,
but they don't like being hugged," said Lucy.

"And they both want to do things
at the same time each day," added Mum.

"Milo does look like he's happy being with us," they all agreed.

The next day Milo woke them up as usual.

He was a brilliant alarm clock.

After breakfast Milo eagerly brought
his favourite ball for Mum to throw...

again and again and again.

Mum loved seeing how happy it made Milo.

When Sam and Lucy played Dragons and Witches,
they made sure both Milo and Monty
had a part they liked.

And Monty always seemed to know what games Milo enjoyed.

"I think Milo loves being with us just as much as Monty," said Mum.

"He just shows it in his own way."